The Great Journey
of
an Anonymous Cat

Luna Jung

The Great Journey of an Anonymous Cat

발 행 | 2024년 5월 24일
저 자 | Luna Jung
펴낸이 | 한건희
펴낸곳 | 주식회사 부크크
출판사등록 | 2014.07.15.(제2014-16호)
주 소 | 서울특별시 금천구 가산디지털1로 119 SK트윈타워 A동 305호
전 화 | 1670-8316
이메일 | info@bookk.co.kr

ISBN | 979-11-410-8653-4

www.bookk.co.kr
ⓒ Luna Jung 2024

The Great Journey
of
an Anonymous Cat

By Luna Jung

I am a 5th-grade student at Burr
Intermediate School.
For all the teachers I had in
Burr Intermediate School.
Especially Ms. Kennedy,
who's the kindest teacher,
Mrs. Fehrenbach, who always
loved reading, and Mrs.
Ferrara, who always took care
of the students.

Author's Words

Reader, if you're expecting any
magical unicorns or fairy, and castles
or something, unfortunately
you are WRONG. There are no
talking animals or any heros with
super powers. This book will show
you a different fantacy story that
you have never seen before. So, good luck.
(The author of this book is half
crazy, just saying.)

Chapters

Prologue

A Homeless Anonymous Cat

Reader, do you know what Anonymous means? It means, "Unknown", or "No settled name". And, the main character of this book is Anonymous.

Everyone called him with many nicknames, like "Alawakazamu" or "Pinkfluffyunicorn" or "SkibiditoiletOhio". Usually, if you don't have a settled name, you may name yourself on your. But reader, he wasn't smart enough to do that. He got a smaller brain than everyone else. So he forgot all the nicknames that people had called him with.

He was a stupid cat, to be honest. But "Stupid" sounds a little mean, so I'll call him "Silly" instead. How about that? I think it sounds better.

Our main character Anonymous cat was a silly cat. He didn't even have a family or home or shelter. So he lived by himself in the alley next to the fish shop. A Thrown-away dusty wooden desk was his home. He lived under it.

Under the wooden desk, there were many precious things for the cat (It basically were thrown away stuffs, but he didn't care.) like tuna cans, a sponge ball, and an old dusty doll. You might wonder how he survives without his parents or owner to take care of her. But reader, it wasn't that hard because of the fish shop settled right next to his alley. The only problem he was supposed to face was the owner of the fish shop, an old woman with a kitchen knife (I don't know, she always was holding it.).

But anonymous cat was very fast. It was an impossible quest to capture a super fast cat as an old woman that can't even stand up without a wooden stick. It might seem like Anonymous is a mean, selfish cat. But he wasn't mean, he only stole a fish that was even smaller than his tiny tail. And most importantly, he needed to survive.

One day, our anonymous cat tried to get a small fish from the fish shop like he always did. For him, it seemed like old owner was sleeping on the chair with a thick-red book on her face and a sharp kitchen knife in her left hand. So he walked over to the fish very comfortably. But unfortunately, he was too silly to notice the old woman reaching her hand to an old dusty wood stick to stand up.

When anonymous grabbed a fish by using his small mouth, that old owner started yelling and chasing him. Anonymous wasn't surprised. Because even though the situation was very unexpected, he was way too silly to be surprised. So like he did always, he jumped to the sky with a fish in his mouth.

"WHEN ARE YOU
GOING TO STOP
STEALING MY FISH?!"
the old woman screamed.
"Meow." The cat said back.
Then, the cat ran away from
the owner.

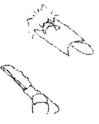

"DON'T EVER COME INTO MY SHOP AGAIN!!!"
The owner shouted. 'Don't ever come into my
shop again'. It was the sentence that she
always said when a small-white cat stole a tiny
fish from her without paying. I guess she isn't
tired of repeating the same sentences
everytime, huh?

Our anonymous's quest was successfully
finished like everyday. He rushed to the dusty
wooden desk with his four small feet. The cat
started eating the fish right after he crawled
under the desk.

The fish didn't taste like the fish he always
ate, but that wasn't important. The only
reason he ate the fish was to survive. It was a
foolish thing to expect a tiny fish that is
smaller than his body to taste good. And like
as always, he finished eating his breakfast.

The sky was not shining because of the sun
for today. The cloud was covering the sun so
tightly that even though it was morning, it
didn't feel like it. The color of the sky was
alike the mixture of blue and gray.

The cat mumbled. "Meow." Then, he quickly

hid himself under the desk. The sky got darker and darker, and little transparent colored water drops started falling down from the sky. And this was the situation that the cat knew was going to happen.

Now reader, you might wonder "If anonymous cat is that silly, how did he know it was going to rain?". Well, here's my answer. "Cats. Hate, hate, HATE, HATE water.", Especially for our anonymous cat, he terribly hated water.

He didn't like the way the raindrops wet his body. So when he tried to stop it by catching, growling, and meowing, obviously none of them work out for him. And that's when he decided to hide from the rain, and learned how to know when the rain is going to come down from the sky to attack him.

"Meow." The cat said. He carefully reached his short arm to get a doll far away from him, but it ended up with wetting his arm with water. "Purr." He whispered. He quickly grabbed his doll with his sharp small nails and put it right next to him. Soon after he picked up the doll, the sponge ball rolled outside to the wet place. "Meow." The cat said. Surprisingly, he didn't try to bring it back to him. All he was doing was staring at the doll, and squishing it with his foot.

Our anonymous cat waited for the water drops to stop falling down from the sky and the sun to show up.

Chapter 1

Rainbow Angel Fish

Our anonymous was feeling anxious because of the rainy weather. He didn't like how he needed to stay under the desk when he didn't want to. So this time, he went out from the desk and started running on the streets. He was too much of an energetic cat to stay under the dusty wooden desk. Would you like to guess where he ran to? Well, the answer is 'I don't know either.'. Reader, he was just running on the streets without knowing where to go. The cat was just following what he sees. Even the weather was getting darker and darker, and he was getting wetter, and wetter. He didn't stop running.

And finally, he arrived somewhere. "Meow."

He said. It was the ocean. As I said, reader. He didn't like water. But for now, him watching the water waving calmly just like him even when the rain was bothering it made the cat felt much comfortable.

Anonymous knew that he came here before because it was very familiar. But unfortunately, he couldn't remember. "Meow." He said. The cat slowly started walking over the sand near the water. It was wet because of the rain, but not musty.

Then, the cat saw something shiny. "Meow.", he mumbled. The cat didn't struggle to go in to the ocean water to check what it was. The water came up to his chin. It was such a beautiful shell that he had never seen, or heard of. Or maybe he did see or hear of it, and just can't remember. When he tried to pick up the shell from the sand, Shiiiii. The big wave came over him and brought him into the deep water. "Meow.", the cat screamed.

Our anonymous was drowning and drowning. He tried to go up, but he couldn't. The weight of the water was way too heavy for him.

'Meow.' He thought under water. Soon, the cat lost all of his power. "Meow." He said for the last time. Then reader, the cat was never found again.

"Hey, hey! Are you dead? Oh wow. I can't believe it! I see how mean god is, I'm definitely not his favorite! I know it!!"

The creaky voice came into the cat's ears. The cat slowly opened his eyes. "Oo, never mind. He is alive still." An unknown thing said. "I'm, an angel of the fish. Nice to meet you, my partner." It said. "Meow." The cat replied. "Well, um. You actually don't need to speak cat language in front of me. No one will notice." The angel said. "Meow." The cat replied once again." Do you even know how to speak?" The angel asked.

"Say meow one more time if you don't, or say something that I can understand if you can." And obviously, the cat said "Meow."

"Un-Belivable!" The angel screamed. "This is not good. How am I going to complete the

quest with this unable to communicate cat?!"
This time, the cat
didn't say anything. He
just started at the angel.

The angel was shiny. It was sparkly like a rainbow, the color of it was very colorful. It was also shaped like a fish. The anonymous cat was not THAT silly to not to notice it's the shape of a fish, so he liked the angel because he knew the shape of it is very familiar for him.

"Meow." The cat said. "Hey, little dude in front of me. I don't care if you can understand me or not. You should just follow me, obey me, and take care of me." The angel said roughly. The cat didn't reply to the angel's words. He was way too busy staring at the angel's sparkly body.

"Meow." The cat said.

"What are you doing? Why are you keep staring at my- oh." The angel said, like it realized something. "You are too busy looking at my beautiful shiny rainbow body! Ahaha, I see, I see." The angel said loudly. "But unfortunately, little cat." Said the fish. "We, gotta go." The cat wasn't thinking, he just followed the fish. The place he woke up wasn't the place that he usually saw. It wasn't the alley, it wasn't the bottom of the ocean, nor the fish shop. It was just a whole white place. Nothing was there except for the angel and the cat. The cat reader, didn't care. He for a short second thought about the alley he lived in, the ocean, and the shiny shell he saw, and his toys. But all of them was forgotten in a second in his head.

Now, everything he was thinking about was the angel of the fish. He always wanted to eat a perfect fish for himself. But he was way too innocent to steal the big, tasty fish from the fish shop back then. And for the cat who never, or who forgot how the 'tasty' fish tastes like, the fish shaped angel that sparks like a rainbow seemed like the best fish to eat in his life, even though he wasn't a perfect grown-up cat.

The anonymous cat reached his little paw up to the angel. And, Snatch. He quickly grabbed the fish. "Ow, ow, OW, OW, OW!! WHAT ARE YOU DOING?" The angel yelled. "Meow." The cat said, opening his mouth. "No, no no no no no. I am not a real fish! I am a gorgeous angel who is shaped like a fish!!" The angel screamed, noticing that the cat was going to eat it. "Let me go! You little stupid cat."

The cat never saw a talking fish. He couldn't understand what the fish was screaming about, but he didn't like loud noises that the fish made. So he gently hit the fish to the ground until it stopped screaming. It's how the cat made the fish die when he lived in the alley. But you gotta know something. The cat, if he kill the fish by eating it, won't be able to leave this white place. Except that he was way too silly to realize that early···. He didn't care about staying in the white place, but this little silly cat didn't know anything about it.

Chapter 2

Sometimes Being Right Is Wrong And Being Wrong Is Right.

"Meow." The cat commented, after checking the angel isn't moving or talking anymore. The cat brought the hand that was grabbing the angel up to his mouth and put it in his small mouth.

"Purr." The cat purred loudly, and spit out the fish. "Meowaoewoaw." The cat groaned. The fish didn't taste like he expected it to. The taste, was alike the raindrops that were salty, and unfresh. The cat moved away from the angel. The body of the angel was still shining like a rainbow. So he just started at the angel until it woke up.

About a minute after our anonymous cat started staring at the angel, something started to make noises. And our cat with sensitive ears knew what were making the sounds. The sounds were very familiar to him, and when you realize what were making the noises, you will know why he was used to it. Because, the sounds were human talking to each other. But it wasn't simple talking. They basically were arguing sounds.

The cat stood up. And finally saw a crowd of people coming closer and closer to the cat.

"I am Right!!"

"No, You are completely wrong!!!"

"You are Useless!!!"

"No, You don't deserve this!!!"

"I didn't kill him!!!"

"Yes You did, LIAR!!!"

The people who were not even able to show their face because of the black shield around them, were fighting each other with many harshful words. Our anonymous cat didn't understand any, Any of the words(Thankfully, because I don't want him to learn any bad things.) they were speaking, but he hated watching them arguing and screaming, so he grabbed the angel and tried to move away.

"What is that Stupid thing over there?!"

"You're stupider! That's a cat!!"

"What the hell is that useless cat doing here?!"

"He's better than you to stay with me fighting!!!"

"What are you doing here, Cat?!" An anxious voice came out. The cat spun his body. "Meow." Then, he gently put down the angel on the ground and stared at them.

"Is 'Meow' all he can say?! How stupid!!!"

"You don't deserve to live!!! DIE, DIE, DIE, DIE!!!!"

Some of the people even screamed out very dangerous words that does not belong to say to others. But they didn't care. Even a little.

"You know what? Let's ask that Stupid cat about it."

"Right!! He is stupid but seems better than you, at least."

People turned their body to the cat. "You, over there. Tell us who's right and wrong." One of them shouted.

"Meow." The cat replied.

And reader, that is how the trial with the most stupid reasons started.

"My honor. He stole my carrots, and killed my cows!!" One of the woman in black started speaking.

"Stop lying, I literally did not!!! My honor. I have my friends with me, and I was with them for whole days!!" The man commented to her with an anxious voice.

"Well, I was with MY father at that day!! And he and I saw you stealing it!!!" The woman screamed.

"My honor, he is such a liar. Please give him a big punishment!!"

"YOU DIRTY LIAR!!!" The man screamed, and roughly walked up to the woman.

"If you ever come near me, I'll cut your-"

"Meow." The anonymous cat started talking.

"Everyone be quiet!! The judge is speaking!!!" Said someone in the crowd. It was completely silent. Now the only one who was allowed to speak was our anonymous cat.

"Meow." The cat said, once more. "Purr." The cat purred. "What is that cat speaking?" The woman said. "Shut up!!! He's speaking!!" The man shouted. "Shhhh." Everyone put their fingers on their own lips. "···,.Meow." The cat spoke. "What?" The woman said again.

"I said SHUT UP!!"

"SHHHHH."

"Meow." The cat said.

The woman was confused. But this time, she didn't say anything. The people that were filled with black were waiting for the cat to speak, to choose who's fault it was.

"My honor, you may speak for them." The man spoke carefully.

"Don't you dare, tell him what to do. He can choose it by himself." One of the crowd commented.

"What? But he isn't speaking anything!" The man said. "Yeah, he's just a stupid cat!!" The woman yelled.

"They are Crazy!! They are believing our

honor as a stupid cat!!! That's illegal!!" The crowd screamed. "We gotta kill them! We gotta kill them!!!"

The crowd slowly came closer and closer to the man and woman. Then, they started punching each other. The sound of the fight was very harmful for everyone. The fight was going on for about 10 minutes. The floor that was white was filled with black color. There was no one left in the crowd. All of them were gone.

"Meow." The cat mumbled. He stared at the black floor that the people were fighting at. The cat was thinking nothing.

Reader, I cannot be sure if you remember or not, but the rainbow angel fish from the last chapter had almost died by the cat. And while the cat and the people were in argument, the angel had already woke up. "Oh no, the cat is going to die!" The angel whispered to himself. But unexpectedly, he did not.

"Hey, cat." The angel said, coming near to the cat. The cat turned over to the angel.

"How⋯, did you do that? I never saw a

person who made them disappear in my angel life." The fish asked, carefully. "Meow." The cat replied. He might have been way too silly to know how. Because all he did was just…, Meowing.

"Well. Nevermind. I was not supposed to ask a stupid cat that doesn't even know how to speak or understand my language to tell me the answer." The angel said.

Chapter 3

The Problem

The angel brought the cat to another place, that was completely not black. "Little buddy. I was planning to never forgive you. Because you put ME in your unfresh mouth…," The fish said. "Meow." The cat replied. "But because of that you succeeded in a problem that no one ever have done before. I will forgive you. Be thankful." The angel mumbled. "Meow." The anonymous cat said. The angel looked at the cat directly. It had two small black eyes like our anonymous cat did. The eyes of the angel were the only part that weren't shiny like his body.

"Meow." The cat whispered. He looked at the fish too.

"Ugh, nevermind." The angel said, turning the head over.

"We need to go. There are problems we need to fix, you know?"

"Like those people that were filled with black... that you made disappear. Little bud, trust me. It won't be easy." The angel was serious. But the cat wasn't. Because he couldn't even understand what the angel was speaking.

"The reason you're here, this stupid white place is because you are the chosen one from the sky, little cat. To go back to your planet, you should finish three tasks." The angel explained.

"And you finished one of them."

"Meow." The cat asked.

"Um, you know? I'm an angel. And angels were always sent to help the chosen people of the quests." The angel said.

"This is the first time that I am the angel

who helps the people.. but yes. Even though you're a stupid cat that doesn't even understand me, I will take you as my partner."

The angel mumbled. "Meow." The cat replied. The angel and the cat walked for a while. When the anonymous cat looked around, all he saw was white color. But the cat wasn't feeling any excitement or anxiousness about it. He was way too silly. "Alright." The angel mumbled. Angel took a deep breath, and touched the cat with its body. A bubble appeared around the cat. "Meow." The cat screamed. "Don't be scared. Nothing's wrong." The angel commented. The bubble slowly rose up and up. It didn't stop moving and rose up and up, until it ended up on something.

Chapter 4

New Friend is Unlocked

The bubble had popped.

"Little dude. You gotta be thankful to me, everyone except for you, would never be able to come to the 'Moon'." The angel said. "Be respectful." "Meow." The cat replied. Reader, the cat was feeling uncomfortable about the place that he was standing on(The moon obviously). Because of the gravity, he couldn't control his body as well as when he was on earth.

Then our anonymous cat remembered the most important thing. It was a doll. The cat always thought about it preciously. He couldn't remember the reason of liking or taking a doll so seriously, but he knew there was something that made him to recognize it important for him. "hey, hello? Are you there? Are you a ghost? Am I talking to an unknown person?" The angel yelled into his ears. ears a little and lift up his face to see angel high up. "Alright, buddy. Here we go." The angel said. "I'll explain only once. You gotta listen well." "The plan is here, this is the planet called Moon. As I said, if you listened well."

"Meow."

"There are ailiens here. You probably are the first per. I mean animal to come to the moon to beat the alien. But there's no helping." The angel said directly. "The aliens don't belong to live in here. They don't deserve to. So, your second challenge would be to make the aliens get out of here, or just kill 'em."

"Meow." The cat replied. "Alright, got it? I'm worried about you, you don't have anything to beat them up." The angel carefully whispered.

"Meow.' The cat said. "Okay, I guess this is the time." The angel said. Right after the angel stopped talking, the UFO that was settled on the area and unknown green creatures came into the cat's eyesight.

"OooOoooOoOOOoooOoOo." One of them said.

"ooooOOoOOooOOoOO? OOooooO." Another of them yelled.

"Meow." The cat said.

"Oo. OoOoOoOOOooOooOOoO."

"OooOOOoOOOoOooOoooOOo?"

"Meow." The cat commented.

"OOOOOO? OOOOOO??"

"Meow."

"Ooo. oooo."

"Purr." The cat said, with an upset face.

"OOOOOO! OOooOoo." The alien said back.
The aliens pulled out the GSG-5 Snipers(It's type of the gun made in Germany.) from their body.

"MeOw." The cat said. His whiskers were high up. The aliens looked at each other.

"OOooOoOoooOo." After one of them saying

something, they quickly put down the snipers.

"Meow." The cat replied.

"OOOOooooOooOoo." The alien said. They slowly moved closer to the cat. 'Oh no, what are they doing? Are they going to eat the cat?!' The angel thought with a worried feeling.

"OoOooOoooOOoooOOoOOo." The alien said, with its hand on the cat's paw.

"Meow." The cat replied politely, with his paw risen up to the alien. They quietly clapped their hands. The shape of the hands were all different. But they probably were thinking all the same. I can be sure.

"OoOoOOoooOOoooOo." One of the alien said.

"Meow." The cat said.

"OooOOoOOoOo."

"Meow." The cat replied. The aliens slowly crawled up to the UFO that was settled on the ground.

"Ba- ba." The aliens said.

"Maw- maw." The cat commented. The UFO disappeared in a second. The cat stared at the spot that the aliens were at for a long time.

"WHAT THE ACTUAL HECK?" The angel screamed, coming out from the rock that he was hiding behind. "How did you make them leave?!!"

"Meow." The cat explained.

"···,Okay. Nevermind. But great job! I'm proud of you." The angel commented.

"Meow."

"'Ight! Let's go to the next place." The angel screamed, cheerfully. The angel went back to work to make a bubble around the cat.
The cat's eyes were still on the place that they were already on.

Reader, even though the aliens were unknown creatures and the cat was too silly to understand them, maybe the cat thought them as part of his friends. It was a first time of a young anonymous cat to have a feeling about it. The cat will maybe be too silly to remember this feeling for the rest of his life, but the cat knew this was the feeling that he mustn't forget for all of the time.

Chapter 5

Size Does Not Matter

The second place that the cat and the angel were at, was under the sea. "Meow." The cat screamed in a traumatized voice. He remembered the time that he got drowned by the ocean waves. "No, it's okay. You'll be able to breath." The fish said, popping the bubble. Deep in the ocean wasn't dark at all. The cat was able to see the sights of his eyes easily, unlike before when he was drowning. "Meow." The cat said in a surprised voice. "Who's there?" Someone spoke carefully. "Meow." The cat replied. "Oh wow, look. Isn't this thing called⋯, a cat?" one of the sirens said. "Purr." The cat commented. "Oh gosh, what are you doing here?" The siren said. "Meow." The cat said. "Well, I'm sorry to do this to you. But we need to make you DIE, 'cause killing is our job." One of them carefully said. "Silly, why would you say that out loud? He's going to run away." Another scolded. "Oops. My bad." "I don't think he's thinking about running away." One siren spoke. "Meow." The cat spoke. "Oh, that's interesting." The siren said, with her hand moving slowly to touch the cat. When the siren was about to touch his head, the cat bit her hand strongly. "Ouch!" The siren screamed. Suddenly all of the sirens turned their head over after hearing a siren screaming.

"That thing just bit me!!" She yelled. The sirens started to scream. "The cat needs to die. The cat needs to die. The cat needs to die." "Meow." The cat replied. The ocean tweaked and rushed like a hurricane after the sirens screamed. "Kill the cat, kill the cat, kill the cat, kill the cat." They yelled. "Meow." The cat screamed and flew away lightly. "Kill the cat, kill the cat, kill the cat." They yelled. The cat was trying to move, but the wave was too strong so he wasn't able to control himself. And that's how the cat randomly went into the innocent whale that was just chilling around. "GulKpt." The whale gulped. "Meow." The cat screamed.

When the cat opened his own two eyes, all he saw was a whole black space with many garbages in it. A strong terrible smell came into his nose. "Meow." The cat whispered silently. The cat decided to move a little. He walked over inside the whale's big body and saw many manythings. There were mysterious stinky boxes that had many shiny things in it, dead fishes bones, slimy creatures that seemed to be alive still.

Reader, if you ever heard or read about the fairytale named Pinocchio, a wooden doll called Pinocchio makes a little fireplace and make the innocent whale cough to escape. Maybe you would think it's going to be perfect for our anonymous cat to do the same thing that Pinocchio had done, but very unfortunately he never ever heard of the Pinocchio story. Even if he did, he wasn't going to be able to remember because he is a silly cat as you know.

So, the cat who almost forgot about the plan already was chilling around the whale like it was a playground. About a minute of him walking around, he found a spike that was stuck in the whale's body.

Our curious anonymous cat was way too curious to just walk across when he saw a big mystery spike stuck in the body. So the cat simply... bit it.

"Gulk gulk gulk." The cat chewed. Something red started to come out from the spot that the spike was on, and the body of the whale started to shake. "Meow." The cat was much more curious now. He screwed the spike and tried to pull it out. The body was shaking more and more, but the cat didn't care.

The big spike was about to come off from the wall of the body. And the cat was very tired. "Akk." The cat whispered. And for him, the last chew of the spike did make the spike come off. The body was very shaky and the cat heard a very huge noise from nowhere.

Then, Boom. The cat was out of the body of the whale so suddenly. The reason that caused it was, the whale.

"Meow." The cat screamed while flying in the sky. He quickly fell down onto the whale's body.

"Gulk gulk gulk," The whale said.

A spike that was in the whale's body came out from the whale's mouth. "Meow." The cat said after checking the spike. "Gulk gulk ugg." The whale replied. "Meow. Meow eomw mew meow." The cat asked. "Gulk." The whale commented. And that is how an anonymous cat and an innocent whale went back under water, my precious reader.

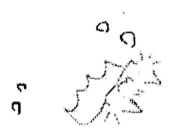

Chapter 6

Eyes and body

The cat and the whale were underwater searching for the sirens. The whale was way too big to check what was going on, so the cat became its eyes. And the cat was way too small and slow to swim all the way, so whale became his body.

"Meow." The cat said.

The whale understood all of the things he said. And he did whatever he told him to do. You know why? It's because for our innocent whale, the anonymous cat was a lifesaver.

"Meow." The cat whispered, seriously. The women-shaped things were sitting around a big rock stacked under the sand. They were talking happily, like nothing wrong happened.

The whale knew that the cat was targeting to kill the sirens by his looking. So, it quickly moved closer and closer to them.

Then,

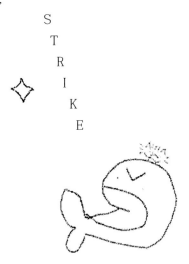

S
  T
   R
    I
     K
      E

The sirens flew up to the sky. The cat was very satisfied, and so did the whale. After they killed(?) the sirens easily, they showed up at the earth and the cat met the angel. "Meow." The cat said, staring at the angel. "Great job again. I saw the sirens flying up to the sky! The sirens die outside the ocean, so I think we're good." The angel replied. But the cat wasn't paying attention on the angel. He was staring at the whale. "Gulk gulk gulk." The whale said. "Meow." The cat whispered, rubbing his paw on the whale's head.

After the few seconds of them talking, the whale disappeared back into the underwater. "Meow." The cat asked. "Well, the next quest can be little struggling for you, but who knows, maybe you're stupid enough to not to feel pain." The fish said. "Meow." The cat said. "Seems like you're ready, huh." The fish whispered. "Well, good luck little dude."

Chapter 7

An Old Doll

This time, our anonymous cat saw the alley he lived before.

"Meow." Someone whispered to him. "Purr."

The cat said back. When he pulled his head up to see who was talking to him, he saw a giant white cat with orange spots on his body and face. He did seem similar to our anonymous cat, but he just couldn't remember who it was. And after a second of thinking, he realized. The cat with orange spots was our anonymous cat's dad. His own father. The cat gasped. "Meow." The father slowly licked anonymous's face. And showed an action to tell the cat to follow him, like it was something he really wanted to show his own son.

The anonymous cat was happy honestly. He thought he never ever had a family before, and it wasn't true. He had a family like everyone. The father cat brought him to the beach. The weather was calm and shiny. There were completely no clouds in the sky and it didn't seem like it was going to rain as well. The anonymous wanted to forget everything and chill with his own father and live happily. Like every story does, happily ever after. Then he thought, reader. 'Is this the ending I want?' The cat realized it was not. But he decided not to break this situation for now. A cat with the orange dots is not anonymous cat's dad.

The father cat and anonymous cat were chilling with a cool ocean wind. The wind was not warm or soft, but it made the cat comfortable. He closed his eyes and relaxed. The father cat was watching anonymous cat with a soft smile. When two cats were planning to go back to the alley, the father cat wasn't speaking anything. Neither did our anonymous cat.

They were just walking together as father and son. The way to get back to the alley was simple. They just needed to cross over the streets and go into the end of the alley so humans don't see them.

The father cat slowly opened his mouth and explained how anonymous cat was like when he was younger. For you, if I write all the things he said. It's going to seem like a bunch of 'Meow's, but for our anonymous cat, it was one of the most precious things he ever heard in his life. It was about whole things that were forgotten in his head. After finishing talking, the father cat slowly handed his son something. It was a doll. The doll wasn't new, so the cat knew about it. Reader, I'm telling you if you forgot. It was the doll that the cat kept under the dusty wooden desk in the alley. And the cat realized everything. The day that his father handed him an old doll right before crossing the road, the anonymous cat almost got hit by a car and his father died while trying to protect him.

"Meow." The anonymous cat cried, telling his father not to go.

But it was too late. A truck hit the father cat....it actually was going to. Except that the anonymous cat threw his body for his father to protect him. And reader, that might be the way that the anonymous cat story ends.

Chapter 8

Someone Who Shall Not Be Forgotten

When our anonymous cat opened his eyes, he felt an extremely strong pain that was impossible to explain. His white fur was red, and all he saw was just a white place and his father.

"Meow." The cat screamed.

The scream made the father cat spin around. And he slowly came over to his son. The father cat stroked a little son that threw his body for him. The pain that the anonymous cat was feeling disappeared completely while his father was stroking him gently. "Meow." The cat said once more.

Reader, this part, the father cat tells our anonymous cat a very important thing to know. Unfortunately, you won't be able to understand what he's talking about because basically, he is a cat. But I'm nice. So I'll translate only the parts that the father cat says, for you.

"You don't belong here." The father cat said, softly. "Seemed like you grew up, hm. I never thought my little son who's scared of everything would be able to throw his body to save me." "Meow." The anonymous cat replied. "Son, last time when it was you who crossed over the street and was about to get hit by the truck, I died and you lost your memories." The father cat said. "I was worried while watching you. What if my son dies. And when you were taken by the waves, I prayed to the skies, to save you." The father cat kept speaking. "The sky gave you three quests to finish, and an angel. While watching you succeed the quests, you won't be able to understand how much I was proud of you."

The anonymous cat felt like he became a baby kitten again. Something was not going right. And the cat knew his father will leave him once again.

"Son, now I can truly trust that you can live bravely, and smartly without me. Now you're an adult cat." The father commented calmly. "After the accident, I know you forgot your name." The cat wasn't ready. He didn't, ever want his father to leave him. "Your name is, Amour. I named you Amour because it means love." The father said. "For this time, don't let others call you anything but Amour." "Meow." The cat said, trying to grab his father. "It's time to go. Son, I love you more than anything. Always be brave, and never give up on anything. And don't be depressed because of me. I will always be with you." The father cat said, gently moving his paw away from Amour. "Meow." The cat cried. His father was gone once more. But the depression ended quickly. The cat decided to let him go. He raised his head up and remembered, that his name is Amour.

Chapter 9

When The Moon Rised Up

Our anonymous.. no, Amour did escape from the white place. The whole quests were finished for him, and that's how he said a simple 'bye' to the angel and got another chance to stay alive. When he went back to his home, which is the alley, the dusty wooden desk, and everything he used to have were settled there with no change. The cat walked up to the doll that his father gave him. Amour was so tired when he just came back from the big adventure, so he slept under the desk with his doll next to his head.

When Amour woke up from his sleep, he realized it was raining. Thankfully he didn't get wet because of the wooden desk, but it was going to be a whole dark space if there was no lantern around him.

Amour closed his eyes and listened to the raindrops falling. When he paid attention to the sound, he could hear another sound aside from the raindrops falling down. It was a walking sound, similar to his. And when he finally opened his eyes, he saw a beautiful black cat running everywhere to find the hiding place.

"Meow." Amour said to the black cat. "Meow." The black cat said, after turning around and seeing Amour. "Meow." Amour asked, to the black cat to come over. And reader, she accepted. Amour letted a black cat search around his house. Even when she touched his precious old doll, he didn't say anything special. He just told her how much this doll is precious to him. The black cat liked hearing the stories. And the story that Amour told her was perfect to make her fall into him.

After some days of Amour living with a black cat in the alley, he could learn everything about her. That her name is Chéri, and she was thrown away in the box by a human owner. And reader, that's how Amour met his soulmate for life. Chéri was a lonely cat. So was Amour. Both of them had the same hobbies too, like visiting the ocean and listening or talking.

3 months after them dating, Amour finally asked Chéri to be his wife by handing a fish to her. And thankfully, Chéri accepted. Both of

the cats always had a happy time together. They always had many romantic times everytime they were together.

When they had a baby kitten, it took a while for Amour to choose a perfect name for his daughter. After some days of him struggling to choose her name, he finally decided to name her Béni, which means 'blessed' in French.

One night of the normal days, three cats were at the beach chilling. The moon was shining in the sky beautifully. Amour had visited the beach many times in his life. But he knew this was one of the few happiest times he's going to have in his life. Because of that he has a complete family, he could be as happy as he could.

Amour's father was the one that Amour always respected. And when he was staring at the moon with his wife and daughter, he remembered days of him and his father chilling at the beach with ocean wind. Amour thought about his father for a second. And he decided to become the best father he could be for his family. Amour was the happiest cat for this time.

They lived happily ever after.

About The Author

Luna Jung

is a Korean woman who moved to US when she was 10. She likes reading, and eating books (Especially fictions) and writings , and enjoys drawing simple illustrations like cats in this book.
The time she decided to write a book was when she was 8, and it was a part of her wishlist. The age that she started to work on this book was when she was 12 years old, in the elementry school at ELA time.

Amour is a fictional character that was created by the author, and he was represented as a cat because the author hoped to break the prejudice about fairytale stories that all the characters are fictional and have magical powers or princesses.